James Smith

Curiosities of Mathematics for the Instruction of Mathematicians

and the benefit of the British Association for the Advancement of Science

James Smith

Curiosities of Mathematics for the Instruction of Mathematicians
and the benefit of the British Association for the Advancement of Science

ISBN/EAN: 9783337406837

Printed in Europe, USA, Canada, Australia, Japan

Cover: Foto ©Andreas Hilbeck / pixelio.de

More available books at **www.hansebooks.com**

CURIOSITIES OF MATHEMATICS

FOR THE INSTRUCTION

OF

MATHEMATICIANS

AND THE BENEFIT OF

THE BRITISH ASSOCIATION FOR THE

ADVANCEMENT OF SCIENCE

BY

JAMES SMITH, ESQ.

MEMBER OF THE MERSEY DOCKS AND HARBOUR BOARD, AND
EX-CHAIRMAN OF THE LIVERPOOL LOCAL MARINE BOARD.

LIVERPOOL
EDWARD HOWELL, CHURCH STREET,

LONDON
SIMPKIN, MARSHALL & CO., STATIONERS' HALL COURT
1870

CURIOSITIES of MATHEMATICS

FOR THE INSTRUCTION

OF

MATHEMATICIANS

AND THE BENEFIT OF

THE BRITISH ASSOCIATION FOR THE

ADVANCEMENT OF SCIENCE

BY

JAMES SMITH, ESQ.

MEMBER OF THE MERSEY DOCKS AND HARBOUR BOARD, AND
EX-CHAIRMAN OF THE LIVERPOOL LOCAL MARINE BOARD.

LIVERPOOL
EDWARD HOWELL, CHURCH STREET,
LONDON
SIMPKIN, MARSHALL & CO., STATIONERS' HALL COURT.
1870

TO THE READER.

FOR many years I have been a regular attender at the Annual Meetings of "The British Association for the Advancement of Science," and it is well known to the Mathematical Members of the Association, that I repudiate the assertion of Mathematicians, that a square exactly equal in superficial area to a given circle cannot be found. On the contrary, I maintain, that by practical Geometry a square equal to a given circle can be constructed, isolated, and exhibited, standing on its equivalent circle ; and this I have proved in a variety of ways, in my published works. I have also proved :—First : That the area of a circle is equal to the sum of the areas of squares on the sides of a right-angled triangle, of which the sides that contain the right angle are in the ratio of 3 to 4, and the middle side the radius of the circle. Second : That the area of a circle is equal to the area of a square on the hypothenuse of a right-angled triangle, of which the sides that contain the right angle are in the ratio of 7 to 1, and the sum of these two sides equal to the diameter of the circle.

The symbol π is adopted to denote the circumference of a circle of diameter unity : and π times the square of the radius $=$ circumference $\times$ semi-radius, in every circle. No *honest* Geometer or Mathematician will dispute, that the equation, $\pi \ (r^2) = (c \times s \ r)$ in every circle, whatever be the value of π.

Hence: If p denote the perimeter of a regular hexagon : c denote the circumference of its circumscribing circle : a denote the area of the circle : and x denote the area of a regular dodecagon inscribed within the circle :—

$$p : c :: x : a$$

$$\therefore \ \pi \left(\frac{p}{6}\right)^2 = \pi \left(\frac{x}{3}\right)$$

But this equation cannot be proved arithmetically with an *indeterminate* value of π : neither can we get this equation from a given arithmetical value of c, with a false value of π.

Let c be represented by any arithmetical quantity, say 360, and it will not be disputed by any *honest* Mathematician, that the circumference of a circle is divided into 360 equal parts, for all practical purposes.

Then :

$$\frac{c}{3\frac{1}{8}} = \frac{360}{3\cdot125} = 115\cdot2 = \text{diameter of the circle} : \frac{\text{Diameter}}{2}$$

$$= \frac{115\cdot2}{2} = 57\cdot6 = \text{radius of the circle} : \frac{\text{Radius}}{2} = \frac{57\cdot6}{2}$$

$= 28\cdot8 = \text{semi-radius of the circle} : 6 \, (r) = (6 \times 57\cdot6) = 345\cdot6 = p$: and $6 \, (r \times s\,r) = 6 \, (57\cdot6 \times 28\cdot8) = 6 \, (1658\cdot88) = 9953\cdot28 = x.$

$$\therefore 3\tfrac{1}{8} \left(\frac{p}{6}\right)^2 = 3\tfrac{1}{8} \left(\frac{x}{3}\right)$$

$$\text{that is, } 3\tfrac{1}{8} \left(\frac{345\cdot6}{6}\right)^2 = 3\tfrac{1}{8} \left(\frac{9953\cdot28}{3}\right)$$

Again :

Divide the diameter of the circle into two parts A B and B C, so that A B shall be to B C in the ratio of 7 to 1.

Then :

$$\frac{\text{Diameter}}{8} = \frac{115\cdot2}{8} = 14\cdot4 = \text{B C} : 7 \, (\text{B C}) = (7 \times 14\cdot4)$$

$100.8 = A\,B$: therefore, $(A\,B^2 + B\,C^2) = (100.8^2 + 14.4^2)$
$= (10160.64 + 207.36) = 10368 = 3\frac{1}{8}\left(\dfrac{A\,B + B\,C}{2}\right)^2$, and

this equation $= a =$ area of the circle.

Hence :

$$\tfrac{24}{25}\,(c) = \tfrac{24}{25}\,(360) = 345.6 = p$$
$$\text{And, } \tfrac{24}{25}\,(a) = \tfrac{24}{25}\,(10368) = 9953.28 = x$$
$$\therefore\ 3\tfrac{1}{8}\left(\tfrac{p}{6}\right)^2 = 3\tfrac{1}{8}\left(\tfrac{x}{3}\right) \text{ as in the previous example.}$$

No other value of π but that which makes 8 circumferences of a circle exactly equal to 25 diameters can produce these results, and it follows, not as an *assumption*, but as a *logical deduction*, that $\tfrac{25}{8} = 3.125$ is the true arithmetical value of the circumference of a circle of diameter unity. It also follows, that $\tfrac{24}{25}\,(3.125) =$ $\dfrac{24 \times 3.125}{25} = \dfrac{75}{25} = 3 =$ the *known* value of the perimeter of an inscribed regular hexagon to a circle of diameter unity. Hence : From the *known* relations that exist between a regular polygon of six sides and a regular polygon of twelve sides inscribed in the same circle, we can ascertain the area of the circle from a given radius, but from no other polygons, whether inscribed or circumscribed to a circle. The reason is obvious. The perimeter of all polygons of more than 6 sides, and the area of all polygons of more than 12 sides are incommensurable.

The Rev. W. Allen Whitworth, Fellow of St. John's College, Cambridge, and formerly Professor of Mathematics in Queen's College, Liverpool, charged me in a Letter he addressed to me, dated November 9th, 1868, with bringing a false accusation against "*recognised Mathematicians*," and in his Letter made the following assertion: " I *know* and *always teach* that the value of π is a finite and determinate quantity ;" and yet, the Reverend gentleman also teaches, that the arithmetical value of π is 3·14159 with a never ending string of decimals. To give his views something like an air of consistency he *asserts*, that the series $1 + \frac{1}{2} + \frac{1}{4} + \frac{1}{8} + \frac{1}{16} + \frac{1}{32} +$ &c. stands for 2.

In the *Liverpool Leader* of August 21, 28, and September 11, 1869, there appeared three Articles from the pen of Mr. Whitworth under the title of "Curiosities of Mathematics. In one of them, in which he introduced my name, he professes to prove that the arithmetical value of π is greater than 3·125. These articles were to be continued, but after waiting several months without seeing any signs of it, I wrote a series of Letters in the *Leader* in which I exposed the fallacy in the premisses, reasoning, and conclusion of Mr. Whitworth. (These Letters appear in my last published work.) To these Letters he never replied, but in April, 1870, I received a curious epistle from him, in which he said :—The series of Articles on "Curiosities of Mathematics" will probably be continued when you (I) have finished writing in the *Leader* under the same title." This led me to make another considerable pause. Still Mr. Whitworth remained silent, and I concluded my series with Letters which will be found in the following pages, and which must speak for themselves.

JAMES SMITH.

BARKELEY HOUSE, SEAFORTH,
1st *August*, 1870.

FROM THE "LIVERPOOL LEADER," JUNE 11TH, 1870.

CURIOSITIES OF MATHEMATICS.

TO THE EDITOR OF THE LIVERPOOL LEADER.

SIR,

The last letter I received from your contributor, the Rev. W. Allen Whitworth, he commenced by saying "the copyright of the articles in the *Leader*, entitled 'Curiosities of Mathematics,' is my property," and he valued each of these articles at twenty guineas. They appeared in the *Leader* of August 21, 28, and September 11th, 1869, without any signature, but with an intimation that they were to be continued. He next observed—"The series will probably be continued when you (I) have ceased inserting advertisements under the same title." It is more that two months since a letter of mine appeared in your Journal, and as yet there is no sign of Mr. Whitworth continuing the series. Has he abandoned his intention? *Nous verrons.* I notice from the announcement in the public papers that he has recently been appointed to the incumbency of Christ Church, Liverpool.

DIAGRAM.

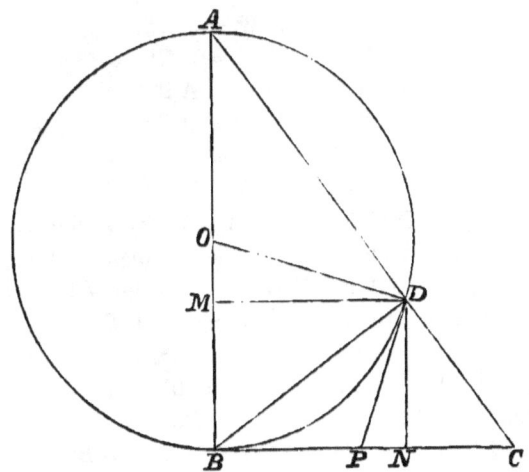

The geometrical figure represented by the diagram may be constructed in the following way:—

Draw the straight line A B and bisect it in O. With O as centre and O A or O B as radius, describe the circle. With A B as perpendicular, describe the right-angled triangle A B C, making B the right angle, and A B to B C in the ratio of 8 to 6. From D the point of intersection between A C the hypothenuse of the triangle A B C and the circumference of the circle, draw the straight line D M perpendicular to A B, and, therefore, parallel to B C. From D draw the straight line D N perpendicular to B C, and, therefore, parallel to A B. Bisect B C in P, and join D P, D B, and D O.

Other methods of construction will suggest themselves to any " reasoning geometrical investigator."

By Euclid: Prop. 31 ; Book 3.

       A D B is a right-angled triangle.

By Euclid: Prop. 4 and Prop. 12 ; Book 2.

$$D O^2 + O A^2 + 2 (O A \times O M) = A D^2$$
$$D P^2 + P B^2 + 2 (P B \times P N) = D B^2$$

By Euclid :   Prop. 47 ; Book I.

$$D M^2 + M A^2 = A D^2$$
$$D M^2 + M B^2 = D B^2$$
$$D O^2 - O M^2 = D M^2$$
$$D P^2 - P N^2 = D N^2$$
$$D N^2 + N B^2 = D B^2$$
$$D N^2 + N C^2 = D C^2$$
$$A D^2 + D B^2 = A B^2$$
$$B D^2 + D C^2 = B C^2$$
$$A B^2 + B C^2 = A C^2$$

By Euclid: Prop. 8 ; Book 6.

The triangles D M A and D M B on each side of D M are similar triangles, and similar to the whole triangle A D B.

The triangles D N B and D N C on each side of D N are similar triangles, and similar to the whole triangle B D C.

$$A B \times A M = A D^2$$
$$A B \times M B = D B^2$$

By Euclid :   Prop. 2, Book 2 ; and Prop. 35, Book 3.

$$(A B \times A M) + (A B \times M B) = A B^2$$

$$(A B \times A O) + (A B \times O B) = A B^2$$
$$(B C \times B N) + (B C \times N C) = B C^2$$
$$(B C \times B P) + (B C \times P C) = B C^2$$

M B N D is a rectangular parallelogram, and it follows that the side N B = the side D M ; and the side D N = the side M B.

Now, B C the hypothenuse of the right-angled triangle B D C, which is also the base of the right-angled triangle A B C, is divided into two equal parts, B P and P C, and into two unequal parts, B N and N C, by construction. Will your contributors, the Rev. W. Allen Whitworth and the Rev. Geo. B. Gibbons—both "*recognised mathematicians* "—favour your mathematical readers with a solution of the following problem ?

PROBLEM.

Find the *exact* arithmetical ratio, *expressed in whole numbers*, between the lengths of B N and N C, the two unequal parts into which B C the hypothenuse of the right-angled triangle B D C, is divided.

I hope Mr. Whitworth and Mr. Gibbons will not think I am asking too great a favour at their hands.

I am, Sir,

Yours obediently,

JAMES SMITH.

BARKELEY HOUSE, SEAFORTH,
June 6th, 1870.

FROM THE " LIVERPOOL LEADER," JUNE 18TH, 1870.

CURIOSITIES OF MATHEMATICS.

TO THE EDITOR OF THE LIVERPOOL LEADER.

SIR,

I sent copies of your last number to upwards of eighty members of the British Association for the Advancement of Science, and have written and posted the following letters :—

J. S. TO THE EDITOR OF THE ATHENÆUM.

SIR,

In this day's number of the *Liverpool Leader*, of which I send you a copy by this post, you will find a letter of mine, in which I give an interesting and important problem for solution. I might have given the following method of constructing the geometrical figure on which the problem is founded.

Let A B be a straight line divided into two unequal parts, A M and M B, in the ratio of 5 to 3. Bisect A B in O, and with O as centre and O A or O B as radius, describe the circle. With A B as perpendicular describe the right-angled triangle A B C, making A B and B C the sides that contain the right angle in the ratio of 4 to 3. A C the hypothenuse of the triangle A B C intersects the circumference of the circle at the point D. Join D O, D M, and D B. From D draw the straight line D N perpendicular to B C, and, therefore, parallel to A B, and join D P.

The problem can be solved without the aid of the *differential calculus* or any other of the higher branches of Mathematics. Will you kindly give the solution of the problem in your next number, which will greatly oblige several of your Mathematical readers, and cannot fail to interest *all* your scientific readers?

I am, Sir,

Yours respectfully,

J. S.

11th June, 1870.

J. S. TO PROFESSOR DE MORGAN.

SIR,

In to-day's number of the *Liverpool Leader*, of which I send you a copy by this post, you will find a Letter of mine, in which I give a problem for solution.

The problem can be solved without the aid of the *differential calculus* or any other of the higher branches of Mathematics. Will you kindly give the solution in the next number of the *Athenæum!* Or, if you prove that the solution is impossible, and thus make my statement to be an untruth, you will, by doing so, prove that "James Smith, of Liverpool, *is nailed by himself to the barn-door as the delegate of miscalculated and disorganised failure.*"

Your dutiful tutelary,

J. S.

11th June, 1870.

J. S. TO THE REV. W. ALLEN WHITWORTH.

SIR,

    In the *Liverpool Leader* of to-day, a copy of which accompanies this communication, you will find a letter of mine, in which I give an interesting and novel problem for solution.

As the Editor of the *Leader* has decided not to insert any further letters on "Curiosities of Mathematics" unless paid for as advertisements, in consideration of your writing a Letter to the *Leader* giving the solution of the problem, to appear in that Journal either of the 18th or 25th of this month, I hereby engage to pay for its insertion as an advertisement.

Yours respectfully,

J. S.

11th June, 1870.

J. S. TO THE REV. GEORGE B. GIBBONS.

MY DEAR SIR,

    I send you by this post a copy of to-day's *Liverpool Leader*, in which you will find a Letter of mine, giving a remarkable and novel problem for solution.

If, in the course of next week, you send me a Letter giving the solution of the problem, I will take care that it is inserted in the *Leader* of the 25th of this month.

I am, dear Sir,

Faithfully yours,

J. S.

11th June, 1870.

J. S. TO E. L. GARBETT.

SIR,

On Saturday last I posted to your address a copy of the *Liverpool Leader* of that day's date. In it you would see a Letter of mine, in which I give a problem. I am prepared to pay you your price (3½d) for a solution of it, and can assure you that I should think I never spent threepence and one-eighth of a penny better.

Yours truly,

J. S.

13th June, 1870.

Whether your contributors, Mr. Whitworth and Mr. Gibbons, do, or do not, favour us with a solution of my problem. I do hope to see some notice taken of it in the next number of the *Athenæum.*

I am, Sir,

Yours obediently,

JAMES SMITH.

BARKELEY HOUSE, SEAFORTH,
June 14th, 1870.

FROM THE "LIVERPOOL LEADER," JUNE 25TH, 1870.

CURIOSITIES OF MATHEMATICS.

TO THE EDITOR OF THE LIVERPOOL LEADER.

SIR,

I have received from the Rev. Geo. B. Gibbons, for insertion in your valuable journal, the following communication, in which he gives what he thinks a solution of the problem, founded on the geometrical figure represented by the diagram in my Letter which appeared in the *Leader* of the 11th inst. :—

G. B. G. to J. S.

My Dear Sir,

Your Letter reached me yesterday, but the newspaper only arrived this day. Using the figure there given :

By similar triangles,

$$\frac{A M}{M D} = \frac{D N}{N C}$$

Or,
$$\frac{A M}{B N} = \frac{M B}{N C}$$

That is :

$$\frac{B N}{N C} = \frac{A M}{M B} \text{ the ratio required.}$$

Again : By the numerical values given

$$\frac{A M}{M D} = \frac{4}{3}$$

$$\frac{B M}{M D} = \frac{3}{4}$$

∴ Dividing one by the other :

$$\frac{A M}{B M} = \frac{16}{9} = \frac{B N}{C N} \text{ the ratio required.}$$

We can easily find the values of all the lines employed.

Put :
$$A M = x$$
$$M B = y$$

Then :

$$x + y = 8$$

But,
$$\frac{x}{y} = \frac{16}{9}$$

Substituting in the first equation the value of y, deduced from the second.

$$x + \tfrac{9}{16}(x) = 8$$
$$\tfrac{25}{16}(x) = 8$$
$$25(x) = 128$$
$$x = 5\cdot12 = A M$$
$$y = \tfrac{9}{16}(x) = 2\cdot88 = M B$$
$$M D = B N = \tfrac{3}{4} A M$$
$$= \tfrac{3}{4}(5\cdot12) = 3\cdot84$$
$$C N = \tfrac{3}{4} B M$$
$$= \tfrac{3}{4}(2\cdot88) = 2\cdot16$$

$$A D^2 = (5 \cdot 12)^2 + (3 \cdot 84)^2 = 40 \cdot 96$$
$$\therefore A D = 6 \cdot 4$$
$$D C^2 = (2 \cdot 16)^2 + (2 \cdot 88^2) = 12 \cdot 96$$
$$\therefore D C = 3 \cdot 6$$

Yours very truly,

G. B. GIBBONS.

WERRINGTON, LAUNCESTON,
    14*th June*, 1870 (*at night*).

Some of the absurdities involved in Mr. Gibbons's supposed solution of the problem will, I think, be self-evident to many of your readers ; but I will deal with these absurdities in a future communication.

I am, Sir,

Yours obediently,

JAMES SMITH.

BARKELEY HOUSE, SEAFORTH,
    June 14*th*, 1870.

CURIOSITIES OF MATHEMATICS (OR OF WHAT?)

SIR,

Having been honoured by Mr. Smith with a special challenge to solve his problem of June 11th, allow me to point out that, by Euclid, B. 6, Prop. 8, the triangle B D C is similar to A B C, and its parts B N D, D N C, are similar to the same.

Wherefore, by Prop. 4, $A B : B C : : B N : N D$

And . . $: : N D . N C$

And as Mr. Smith makes $A B : B C : : \quad 4 \quad : \quad 3$

By B. 5, def. 10, $B N : N C$ in the duplicate ratio of $4 : 3$—that is, $16 : 9$.

Now, it is really too bad to tax the time of two clergymen— "recognised Mathematicians" or not—with this as a "curiosity ;" and having said so, and answered it for them, I will beg to substitute one worthy their calculation.

7, MORNINGTON ROAD, N.W.,
16th June, 1870.

DEAR SIR,

I am not surprised at your flood of replies to Mr.
Smith's mere schoolboy "problem." Having received both it and a
Letter from him, without knowing what the Rev. Mr. Whitworth's
"curiosity" of last year might have been, I thought well to suggest
one, but should not feel called on to spend anything on publishing
it. If, after Mr. Smith is settled, you like to introduce this as an
independent "curiosity," with my name, or (preferably) without, this
amended version will work.

I am, Sir,
Yours truly,
E. L. GARBETT.

A "CURIOSITY OF MATHEMATICS," SUGGESTED TO THE REV. W. ALLEN WHITWORTH.

A testator left a property to be thus employed, after being turned
into money :—His executors were to advertise in a certain number
of newspapers of the largest circulation, requesting the Archbishop
of the province to answer these three questions. The last chapter of
Scripture that contains these words, " If any man have an ear let him
hear," ends, he said, with a riddle concerning a "name," whose
Letters, taken as numerals in the arithmetic of that day, were to
notate a given number. The Archbishop to be asked to state (1)
whether the New Testament contained any name—that is, any
noun in the nominative case (whether substantive, adjective, or
participle)—that answered the said riddle ; (2) whether it contained
more than one ; and (3) what the name, if any, was, or the names,
if more than one, were. On his Grace answering publicly all three
questions, the advertising was to cease, the remaining money to be
laid up six months, and then applied to such purpose as the said
Archbishop might direct, unless any of his answers had meanwhile
been proved false, but in that case paid to the person proving it so.
And unless or until his Grace might answer all three questions, the
advertising was to be repeated daily till a certain sum named was

expended. On this occurring the same questions were thenceforth to be put to the Roman Catholic Archbishop alone, in the same manner, and with all the same conditions ; and unless or until he might answer, the advertisements were to continue till the whole money were exhausted therein.

On execution of this will commencing, the Protestant Archbishop set a clerk on Bruder's " Concordantiæ Noir Testamenti " (Leipsic, 1842), to examine every noun occurring in the nominative, beginning from A, working 8 hours per diem. The average time to find and examine each was 3 minutes. Meanwhile, the daily cost of repeating the question was £5. Presently he answered question 1 ; but before he could answer 2 or 3, and when it appeared the next day would have completed the work, the day came that, in accordance with the will, the enquiry had to be transferred to the Romish prelate. He, guessing that the Protestant had probably began alphabetically and used the above Concordance, set two clerks on the same book, but beginning from the end, or rather the last possible noun (as no word containing Y or W could answer, the numeral meaning of either of these Letters being too high). As these clerks checked each other, and were paid by job instead of time, their joint progress was just thrice that of the Protestant ; and presently, without their going through the book, their master was enabled both to confirm the answer given to question 1, and answer 2 and 3. After six months, none of these answers being disproved, he obtained the disposal of the remaining legacy.

PROBLEM.

Without knowing the sum left, or that ultimately thus applied, what would have been saved from the advertising expense had the Protestant got through his work a day sooner ?

E. L. GARRETT.

———

SIR,

Mr. James Smith, under this heading, propounds in your columns of Saturday last (p. 245) a "problem," addressed to Mr. Whitworth and Mr. Gibbons ; and as he has done me the honour to send me a copy of your paper, I presume he wishes for

an answer from me. The "problem" is not a very formidable one,
any tyro can see that from the similarity of the triangles,

$$B N : N C :: A D : D C :: A B^2 :: B C^2$$

i.e., by the data : : 64 : 36 : : 16 : 9.

Your obedient Servant,

ALEX. ED. MILLER.

24, OLD BUILDINGS, LINCOLN'S INN,
June 13*th*, 1870.

FROM THE "LIVERPOOL LEADER," JULY 2ND, 1870.

CURIOSITIES OF MATHEMATICS.

TO THE EDITOR OF THE LIVERPOOL LEADER.

SIR,

The past week has been very prolific of correspondence
on the above subject. I give the following, which I think will be
both amusing and instructive to your scientific readers :—

E. L. GARBETT TO J. S.

DEAR SIR,

As I pointed out to the Editor of the *Liverpool
Leader*, on receiving his paper of June 11, nothing more is necessary
to prove the ratio of B N to N C, which you demand on page 245,
than to observe that the parts A B D, B D C, into which you divide
A B C, are (by Euclid, Book 6, Prop. 8) similar thereto ; and again,
those of B D C—viz., B N D, D N C—are, for the same reason,
similar to the same. As you made A B : B C :: 4 : 3, this is also
(by Prop. 4 of same book) the ratio of the legs containing the right
angle in any of these 5 triangles. As B N : N D :: 4 : 3, and also
D N : N C :: 4 : 3 ; therefore, B N : N C in the duplicate ratio of
4 to 3,—that is, as 16 to 9.

This is also the ratio of A M to M B, and of A D to D C, in

the figure constructed, as directed on page 245. But you now, on page 262, describe a different figure. Instead of finding M, as before, by dropping D M perpendicular to A B, you tell us this line is divided into A M, M B in the ratio of 5 to 3 ; in which case M D will not be a perpendicular—though this shifting of the point M nowise affects your problem, for which O, M, and P, are wholly superfluous. It makes your figure a new one, containing only six right-angled triangles, while that of last week contained nine.

I cannot see why anyone should be at expense to advertise proofs of mistakes like these, in which any schoolboy advanced beyond Book I. or II would correct you ; and how could Professor De Morgan ask the *Athenæum* to cover therewith paper due to its readers' information or amusement ?

As it appears a clergyman began, and another attends to. the Liverpool "Curiosities of Mathematics," I gave the Editor, af.er answering you, a new " Curiosity founded on your late Catholic will case," and the subject of your late 666-problemed friend. He can bring that forward whenever he may think fit. Meanwhile, I expect you will advertise whatever those you publicly called on may have had to say to your problem.

I am, Sir,
Faithfully yours,
E. L. G.

7, MORNINGTON ROAD, N.W.,
   20th June, 1870.

J. S. TO E. L. GARBETT.

DEAR SIR,

   I am in receipt of your favour of yesterday, for which I thank you, as it has led me to detect an omission in my letter on page 262 of the *Liverpool Leader*.

In giving the method of constructing the geometrical figure on which the problem is founded in the letter to the *Athenæum*, the concluding sentence should have run thus :—*Bisect B C in P*, and from D draw the straight line D N perpendicular to B C, and, therefore, parallel to A B, and join D P. It is hardly conceivable that you could be ignorant of the fact, that the omission of the words " *bisest B C in P* " was a mere *lapsus*.

Assuming you to have made this correction, may I ask you to construct two diagrams—one by the method given on page 245 of the *Liverpool Leader*, and the other by the method given on page 262 of that Journal. The geometrical figures represented by the two diagrams will be similar in all respects, and I defy you to prove the contrary, unless you are prepared to prove " Euclid at Fault" in his theorem : Prop. 31, Book 3. It is sheer nonsense to say that by the method of construction given on page 262 we get a figure in which M D is not perpendicular to A B ; and worse than nonsense to say :— " Though this shifting of the point M nowise affects your problem, for which O, M, and P are wholly superfluous."

Referring to the diagram in my letter in the *Liverpool Leader* of the 11th inst., the following things are self-evident :—

B P + P N = B N ; and, P C — P N = N C ; and B N + N C = 2(B P) = B C, by construction.

M D = B N, and M B = D N, for they are opposite sides of the parallelogram M B N D ; and it follows, that M D + N C = B C ; but it does not follow that A M D and A B C are similar triangles, or that A M D and D N C are similar triangles.

I have received a letter from the Rev. Geo. B. Gibbons, giving a supposed solution of my problem. He, of course, intended it for insertion in the *Liverpool Leader*, and it will appear in next Saturday's number. I may tell you that he makes the ratio between B N and N C the same as you do—that is, as 16 to 9 ; but you are both wrong.

I know that 666 is the number of the Apocalyptic beast, but I do not know what you mean when you speak of " the subject of your (my) late 666-problemed friend."

Now, $24 + 7 = 31$; and $24 - 7 = 17$; and B N : N C : : 31 : 17.
Proof: Let B P = 666.

Then : Because B C is bisected in P, $2(B P) = 2(666) = 1332 = B C$.

Hence : $B P + \frac{7}{24}(B P) = 666 + 194\cdot25 = 860\cdot25 = B N$

And : $P C - \frac{7}{24}(P C) = 666 - 194\cdot25 = 471\cdot75 = N C$

But : $860\cdot25 : 471\cdot75 : : 31 : 17 :$

∴ B N : N C : : 31 : 17.

In the following way you might have made B N : N C :: 30 : 18, and with a much greater show of plausibility than by your 16 to 9 ratio.

$$\text{Let } A B = 8$$

Then : $\frac{3}{4}(A\,B) = \frac{3}{4}(8) = B\,C$, by construction $= 6$.

$\frac{3}{8}(A\,C) = \frac{3}{8}(8) = M\,B$, by construction $= 3$.

A B C and D N C are apparently similar triangles, and D N = MB, by construction.

$\therefore \frac{3}{4}(D\,N) = \frac{3}{4}(3) = 2\cdot25 = N\,C$, and $B\,C - N\,C = 6 - 2\cdot25 = 3\cdot75 = B\,N$, and $\frac{3\cdot75}{2\cdot25}$ is a ratio.

Multiply the two terms of this ratio by 8, and we get the equivalent ratio $\frac{30}{18}$. But, B N is not to N C in the ratio of 30 to 18.

The concluding sentence of the last paragraph of your letter shall have my attention.

I am, Sir,

Faithfully yours,

J. S.

Barkeley House, Seaforth,
June 21st, 1870.

————

E. L. GARBETT to J. S.

Dear Sir,

I have yours of yesterday, and the only thing it calls on me to answer is. that by " your 666-probleined friend " I meant him whose book you sent to Professor De Morgan, and of whom the latter said that " if there were anything in Christianity he would have been no fool."[*] I forget his name, he who published two volumes, therefore more than 666 puzzlements about the beast's name, and never settled more than a bishop what that name was after all.

* This refers to the late Dr. Thom of Liverpool, author of a work entitled :—"The number and names of the Apocalyptic Beasts," but this was not the book I sent to Professor De Morgan. Dr. Thom was a personal and intimate friend of mine, and was well known and highly respected in my native town. Professor De Morgan made Dr. Thom into a paradoxer as well as myself, and coupled and devoted a whole chapter to us, in his Budget of Paradoxes." J. S.

You can construct your two diagrams on the front and back of tracing paper as large as the docks if you can get it (I advise that the circle should be only 3½ diameters round), and, when you make M correspond in both, I will procure and pay you, in 3½ days, 3¼ times the gold in Solomon's revenue. But, till then, I cannot pay one more postage on the matter,—not one, observe,—and you owe me 3½d. for showing the ratio of B N to N C.

Yours faithfully,

E. L. G.

7, MORNINGTON ROAD,
   22nd June, 1870.

——— ——

J. S. TO E. L. GARBETT.

SIR,

Referring to the geometrical figure represented by the diagram in my Letter in the *Liverpool Leader* of the 11th instant, let c denote the circumference of the circle; let p denote the perimeter of an inscribed regular hexagon; let a denote the area of the circle; and let x denote the area of a regular dodecagon inscribed within the circle.

Now, Sir, if you be "a reasoning geometrical investigator," a Christian, and "no fool," you will—with the information I have given you in my last communication—perform the following feats:—

First: Find the exact arithmetical value of the circumference of a circle of diameter unity.

Second: Prove that $D N : D P :: p : c$.

Third: Prove that $D N : D P :: x : a$.

Faithfully yours,

J. S.

BARKELEY HOUSE, SEAFORTH,
   23rd June, 1870.

The Rev. Geo. B. Gibbons to J. S.

My Dear Sir,

I duly received yesterday the *Liverpool Leader* of 18th June. I notice a difference between the presented "constructions" in the Papers of 11th and 18th June. In the former, M is fixed by your giving D M perpendicular to A B. In the latter, M is fixed by the given ratio $\frac{A M}{B M} = \frac{5}{3}$. The rest of the construction being the same in both, these fixtures will not place M in the same point. D M is no longer perpendicular to A B. For, if D M be perpendicular to A B, making A M = 5 and B M = 3, we get A M × B M = D M^2, or 15 = D M^2, — that is, D M = $\sqrt{15}$. But, $\frac{C B}{A B} = \frac{D M}{A M} = \frac{\sqrt{15}}{5}$ not $\frac{3}{4}$.

I sent you the solution you asked, according to conditions of 11th June, in *Liverpool Leader*, and then $\frac{A M}{B M} = \frac{16}{9}$.

Yours truly,

G. B. G.

Werrington, Launceston,
22nd June, 1870.

—————

J. S. to the Rev. Geo. B. Gibbons.

My Dear Sir,

I am in receipt of your favour of the 22nd instant, which has had my careful attention. In giving a method of constructing the geometrical figure on which my problem is founded in the Letter to the Editor of the *Athenæum*, as given in the *Leader* of the 18th instant, the last sentence should have run thus:— Bisect B C in P, and from D draw a straight line D N perpendicular to B C, and therefore, parallel to A B, and join D P. I can hardly conceive it possible that you can have a doubt in your mind as to the fact, that the omission of the words, *bisect B C in P*, was a mere *lapsus*.

I admit that there is "a difference between the presented 'construction' in the papers (*Leader*) of 11th and 18th inst. ;" but, whether the construction be made by one method or the other, the result will be the same—that is to say, if diagrams be drawn by both methods, the geometrical figures so constructed will be similar in all respects. You say:—"In the former, M is fixed by your giving D M perpendicular to A B. In the latter, M is fixed by the given ratio $\frac{A M}{B M} = \frac{5}{3}$. The rest of the construction being the same in both, these fixtures will not place M in the same point. D M is no longer perpendicular to A B." In this you are decidedly wrong. "*If you can't see it I can't help it, but the fact remains notwithstanding.*" You next observe :—"For, if D M be perpendicular to A B, making A M = 5 and B M = 3, we get A M × B M = D M² or 15 = D M²— that is, D M = $\sqrt{15}$." Now, I admit that, by Euclid (Prop. 13, Book 6), D M is a mean proportional between A M and B M, and = $\sqrt{15}$ when A M + B M = A B = 8. But your conclusion, "$\frac{C B}{A B} = \frac{D M}{A M} = \frac{\sqrt{15}}{5}$ not ¾," is a gross absurdity, for, C B : A B : 6 : 8, by construction.

Referring to the geometrical figure represented by the diagram in my Letter in the *Liverpool Leader* of the 11th instant, it is self-evident that B N + N C = B C ; and because B C is bisected in P, B P + P N = B N, and P C — P N = N C. You may tell me that these are simply truisms, whatever be the value of P N. Granted ! But can you find the exact arithmetical value of P N ? Can you prove that B N + N C = 6, when A B = 8, by your analogy or proportion, B N : N C :: 16 : 9 ? Pray, Sir, let there be no shirking of these questions !

Let B C = 48.

Then : $\frac{48}{2}$ = 24 = B P

$\frac{7}{24}$ (B P) = $\frac{7 \times 24}{24}$ = 7 = P N

B P + P N = 24 + 7 = 31 = B N

P C — P N = 24 — 7 = 17 = N C

∴ B N : N C :: 31 : 17

∴ B N + N C = 31 + 17 = 48 = the given value of B C.

Again :   Let B C = 50.

Then : $\frac{50}{2}$ = 25 = B P

$$\frac{7}{24}(\text{B P}) = \frac{7 \times 25}{24} = 7{\cdot}291666... = \text{P N}$$

B P + P N = 25 + 7·291666. . = 32·291666...`= B N

And, B N : N C : : 31 : 17

But, 31 : 17 : . 32·291666... : 17·708332...

∴ N C = 17·708332...

∴ B N + N C = 32·291666... + 17·708332... = 49·999998...

and is less than 50, the given value of B C ; but it does not follow, that B N is NOT to N C in the ratio of 31 to 17.

Now, if, in the right-angled triangle A B C the sides A B and B C be 8 and 6, a straight line drawn from the right angle B perpendicular to its opposite side A C will divide the triangle A B C into two similar triangles A D B and BDC, and these triangles will be similar to the whole triangle A B C, and B D will be a mean proportional between AD and DC ; but it does not follow, because the two sides that contain the right angle in a right-angled triangle are in the ratio of 8 to 6, that under *all* circumstances a straight line drawn from the right angle perpendicular to its opposite side will divide the triangle into two similar triangles.

For example : Let A B = 8. Then : $\frac{4}{5}$(8) = 6·4 = A D : $\frac{3}{4}$(A B) = $\frac{3}{4}$(A D) = 4·8 = B D : $\frac{3}{4}$(B D) = 3·6 = D C (in your letter of the 14th inst. you make A D = 6·4 and D C = 3·6), and B D C is a right angled triangle, of which the sides B D and D C, which contain the right angle, are in the ratio of 8 to 6 : therefore, by Euclid, Prop. 47, Book 1, (B D² + D C²) = (4·8² + 3·6²) = 23·04 + 12·96) = 36 = B C² ; therefore, $\sqrt{36}$ = 6 = B C. Now, D N = M B = 3 ; and B N = M B = $\sqrt{15}$ when A B = 8 ; and by Euclid, Prop. 13, Book 6, D N is a mean proportional between B N and N C,—that is B N : N D : : N D : N C ; or, $\sqrt{15}$: 3 : : 3 : N C. But, $\sqrt{15}$: 3 : : 3 : $\sqrt{5\cdot4}$, and you will find that this would make B C greater than 6, which is impossible. Surely it cannot be necessary to proceed further. Well, then, from what precedes, the following questions arise :—Is it Euclid that is at fault ? Or, is it mathematics that are at fault ? Or, is geometry " *a mockery, a delusion, and a snare ?*"

The fact is, Euclid and mathematics are both at fault. Euclid's Propositions 8 and 13, Book 6, are not of general and universal application in practical geometry. These Propositions are inconsistent with each other, and both are inconsistent with many other Propositions of Euclid when tested by "*that indispensable instrument of science, Arithmetic.*"

I presented you with a copy of my work, " The Geometry of the Circle ;" and, in conclusion, may refer you to Diagram 8, and my Letter to the Rev. Professor Whitworth, page 140. I may also refer you to the Letters to J. M. Wilson, Esq., pages 334, 335, &c.

Faithfully yours,

J. S.

June 25th, 1870.

I think I have put your contributor, the Rev. Geo. B. Gibbons, in a fix, out of which he will find it difficult to wriggle.

I am, Sir,

Yours obediently,

JAMES SMITH.

BARKELEY HOUSE, SEAFORTH,
June 27th, 1870.

FROM THE "LIVERPOOL LEADER," JULY 9TH, 1870.

CURIOSITIES OF MATHEMATICS.

TO THE EDITOR OF THE LIVERPOOL LEADER.

SIR,

The Editor of the *Athenæum* and Professor De Morgan declined to solve the problem given in my Letter in the *Leader* of the 11th June, as requested in my communications to them of that date. This led me to write them again.

J. S. TO THE EDITOR OF THE ATHENÆUM.

SIR,

In your publication of this day I find no reference to the problem I gave in my Letter in the *Liverpool Leader* of the 11th

4

inst., a copy of which I sent you. The following is the solution of the problem, and proves the necessity of including "arithmetical considerations" in the study of Geometry.

Let $AB = 8$.

Then: $BC = \frac{3}{4}(AB)$, by contruction $= 6$.

But: BC is bisected in P.

$\therefore BP = PC = 3$.

Hence: $BP + \frac{7}{24}(BP) = BN$, and, $PC - \frac{7}{24}(PC) = NC$.

$\therefore BN = 3\cdot875$, and, $NC = 2\cdot125$.

$\therefore BN + NC = 3\cdot875 + 2\cdot125 = BC = 6$.

$\therefore \dfrac{3\cdot875}{2\cdot125}$ expresses the ratio between BN and NC.

Multiply the two terms of this ratio by 8, and we obtain the equivalent ratio $\frac{31}{17}$; and it follows, that BN is to NC in the ratio of 31 to 17. The ratio is expressed in whole numbers, and with arithmetical exactness. Q. E. D.

Now, Sir, conceive a dozen of the Members of the Royal Society of England, a dozen Members of the Royal Institute of France, and a dozen of the leading Members of the British Association for the Advancement of Science, with Professor De Morgan (the greatest Mathematician in Europe, according to my correspondent R. F. Glaister, Esq.) as their secretary, assembled in solemn conclave to solve my problem. They would no doubt decide that the solution of the problem is impossible, aye, and would probably say, just as impossible as to square the circle, or find the *exact* ratio of diameter to circumference in a circle.

But, Sir, I have given you the solution of the problem, and no Mathematician in the world can controvert it ; and if you fail to take the earliest opportunity of giving the problem and its solution in the columns of the *Athenæum*, will you play the part of an honest scientific journalist ? If you find my solution to be irrefragable and decline to admit the fact, what will you be ? Do you suppose that the *Athenæum* can for any length of time stifle scientific truth, and "bolster up" false systems, by maintaining a dogged silence with regard to unpalatable truths, because they happen to jar with long-cherished prejudices ? *Magna est veritas, et prævalebit.*

Yours respectfully,

18th June, 1870.   J. S.

J. S. to PROFESSOR DE MORGAN.

SIR,

In the *Liverpool Leader* of last week I gave an interesting and novel problem for solution, and I sent you a copy of the paper. As I have no doubt you found yourself incompetent to comply with the request I made in my Letter to you of the 11th inst., I now give you the solution of the problem. (See the foregoing Letter.)

Now, Sir, if you can " upset " my solution of the problem and won't, what are you ? If you find it to be irrefragable and hesitate to admit the fact, what will you be ?

I should like to see you grapple with this Letter in a final supplementary chapter to your " Budget of Paradoxes."

Your dutiful tutelary,

J. S.

18*th June*, 1870.

The Rev. Professor Whitworth and the learned Professor De Morgan were too cunning to be caught in the trap I set for them in my Letter in the *Leader* of the 11th June last. Not so Gibbons, Garbett, and Miller, and I may tell you that another gentlemen well known as the recognised " Mathematical authority" of Liverpool swallowed the bait, and was caught in the trap. All these gentlemen are agreed in making B N to N C (see diagram) in the ratio of 16 to 9 ; but they all fail to perceive, that if orthodox theories were true, the solution of my problem would be an utter impossibility. Professor De Morgan's Mathematical knowledge will not enable him to solve the problem on orthodox theories, but his temper will not permit him to take the humiliating step of admitting it.

If De Morgan have any self-respect, he will either prove my solution of the problem to be fallacious, or withdraw, and apologise for, the scurrilous attacks he has made upon me from time to time in the columns of the *Athenæum*.

If I were to attempt to give my problem and its solution in Section A of the British Association at its forthcoming Meeting, I have no doubt I should be grossly insulted, as I have been over and over again in the last ten years, when I have submitted Papers which I was wishful to read in that Section.

In the *Athenæum* of September 9, 1865, or in the Transactions of the British Association for that year, you will find the President's (Professor Phillips) inaugural address, which concludes as follows :—

"Here, indeed, is the stronghold of the British Association. Wherever and by whatever means sound learning and useful knowledge are advanced, there to us are friends. Whoever is privileged to step beyond his fellows on the road of scientific discovery will receive our applause, and, if need be, our help. Welcoming and joining in the labour of all, we shall keep our place among those who clear the roads, and remove the obstacles from the paths of science ; and whatever be our own success in the rich fields that lie before us, however little we may now know, we shall prove that, in this our day, we knew at least the value of knowledge, and joined hands and hearts in the endeavour to promote it."

I shall leave it to your readers to reconcile the fulsome and extravagant professions of Professor Phillips, with the common practice of the Association. I know from personal experience, and from the treatment I have seen others meet with in Section A of the British Association, that, if a gentlemen offer to read a Paper, and his views are known to jar with the long-cherished prejudices of Mathematicians, his Paper will certainly be rejected ; and if he attempt to take part in a discussion on a Paper, he will as certainly be insulted.

I had written so far when this day's *Leader* came into my hands. On reading the erratum of Mr. E. L. Garbett, I was led to address the following short letter to that gentleman :—

SIR,

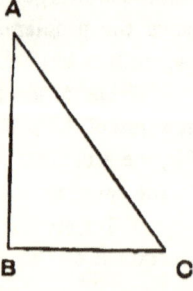

A B C represents a right-angled triangle, of which B is the right angle.

If $AB = \eta + \pi' + \omega$

And $AC = s' + \xi' + \chi'$

How many times is AB^2 contained in the sum of the squares of the three sides of the triangle ?

This cannot be a "puzzlement" to you, or to a bishop, and I shall not object to pay 2d. postage for an answer to the question.

Faithfully yours,

J. S.

Surely Mr. E. L. Garbett is sufficient of "a Christian and a Gentleman" to answer my question! Will he expound my "riddle?" *Nous verrons !*

I am, Sir,

Faithfully yours,

JAMES SMITH.

BARKELEY HOUSE, SEAFORTH,
    2nd July, 1870.

FROM THE "LIVERPOOL LEADER," JULY 16TH, 1870.

CURIOSITIES OF MATHEMATICS.

TO THE EDITOR OF THE LIVERPOOL LEADER.

SIR,

For several weeks past, Letters of mine have appeared in your valuable journal under the above title, and with this communication I shall conclude the series.

Again, referring to the geometrical figure represented by the diagram in my Letter in the *Leader* of the 11th June :

Let A B the diameter of the circle = 8.

Then : B C = $\frac{3}{4}$(A B), by construction = 6.

    A O + O M = A M = $\frac{5}{8}$ (A B), by construction 5

    M B = $\frac{3}{4}$(O B), by construction = 3.

But   B C is bisected in P.

    $\therefore$ B P = P C = M B = 3.

        By Euclid : Prop. 8, Book 6.

    A B $\times$ A M = 8 $\times$ 5 = 40 = A D^2

    $\therefore$ A D = $\sqrt{40}$.

    A B $\times$ M B = 8 $\times$ 3 = 24 = D B^2

    $\therefore$ D B = $\sqrt{24}$

    A M $\times$ M B = 5 $\times$ 3 = 15 = M D^2

    $\therefore$ M D = $\sqrt{15}$.

By Euclid: Prop. 47, Book 1.

$A B^2 + B C^2 = 8^2 + 6^2 = 64 + 36 = 100 = A C^2$

$\therefore \sqrt{100} = 10 = A C$; that is $= A D + D C$

$A D^2 + D B^2 = \sqrt{40}^2 + \sqrt{24}^2 = 40 + 24 = 64 = A B^2$

$\therefore A B = \sqrt{64} = 8$

$B C^2 - D B^2 = 6^2 - \sqrt{24}^2 = 36 - 24 = 12 = D C^2$

$\therefore D C = \sqrt{12}.$

Now, $D N = M B$ for they are opposite sides of the parallelogram $M B N D$; and for the same reason $M D = B N$.

Hence: $\frac{7}{24} (B P) = \frac{7}{24} (3) = \frac{7 \times 3}{24} = \frac{21}{24} = ·875 = N P.$

$\therefore N P + P B = ·875 + 3 = 3·875 = N B.$

By Euclid: Prop. 47, Book 1.

$D N^2 + N B^2 = 3^2 + 3·875^2 = 9 + 15·015625 = 24·015625 = D B^2$, and is greater than 24.

But, $D N^2 + N P^2 = 3^2 + ·875^2 = 9 + ·765625 = 9·765625 = D P^2.$

$\therefore \sqrt{9·765625} = 3·125 = D P.$

By Euclid : Prop. 12, Book 2.

$D P^2 + P B^2 + 2 (P B \times P N) = B D^2$

$\therefore 3·125^2 + 3^2 + 2 (3 \times ·875)$

$= 9·765625 + 9 + 5·25 = 24·015625$

$= D B^2$, and is greater than 24.

By Euclid, Prop. 8, Book 6, $M D = \sqrt{15}$ when A B the diameter of the circle $= 8$; and by Euclid, Prop. 13, Book 6, M D is a mean proportional between $A M$ and $M B$; therefore, $A M : M D :: M D : M B$—that is, $5 : \sqrt{15} :: \sqrt{15} : 3$; therefore, $M B = 3$. By Euclid, Prop. 13, Book 6, N D is a mean proportional between B N and N C; therefore, $B N : N D :: N D : N C$—that is, $\sqrt{15} : 3 :: 3 : \sqrt{5·4}$; therefore, $N C = \sqrt{5·4}$. But, $\sqrt{15} = 3·872...$, and $\sqrt{5·4} = 2·323...$; therefore, $B N + N C = 3·872... + 2·323... = 6·195...$ and is greater than $B N + N C$—that is, greater than 6, the known value of the line B C when $A B = 8$.

Again : By Euclid, Prop. 13, Book 6, B D is a mean proportional between A D and D C : and by Euclid, Prop. 8, Book 6, $A D = \sqrt{40}$, and B D = $\sqrt{24}$ when A B = 8 ; therefore, A D : B D : : B D : D C —that is, $\sqrt{40}$: $\sqrt{24}$: $\sqrt{24}$: $\sqrt{14\cdot4}$; therefore, D C = $\sqrt{14\cdot4}$. But, $\sqrt{40}$ = 6·325... and $\sqrt{14\cdot4}$ = 3·794...; therefore, A D + D C = 6·325... + 3·794... = 10·119..., and is greater than A D + D C— that is, greater than 10, the known value of the line A C when A B = 8, and B C = 6.

The Rev. Geo. B. Gibbons, in his Letter of the 14th June, which appeared in the *Leader* of the 25th June, makes A D = 6·4 and D C = 3·6, when A B = 8 ; and, by Euclid, Prop. 13, B D is a mean proportional between A D and D C ; therefore, A D × D C = 6·4 × 3·6 = 23·04 = B D², and is less than 24, the value of B D² as ascertained by Euclid, Prop. 8, Book 6.

According to Gibbons, Garbett, Miller, and my Liverpool friend, B N is to N C in the ratio of 16 to 9.

Let B C the hypothenuse of the right-angled triangle B D C = 25.

If these gentlemen be right in their ratio, then, according to common sense, B N = 16 and N C = 9. By Euclid, Prop. 2, Book 2, (B C × B N) + (B C × N C) = (25 × 16) + (25 × 9) = (400 + 225) = 625 = B C² ; therefore, $\sqrt{625}$ = 25 = B C. But, when the whole line B C = 6, I have proved that B N is to N C in the ratio of 31 to 17, making B N = 3·875 and N C = 2·125 ; and by Euclid, Prop. 2, Book 2, (B C × B N) + (B C × N C) = (6 × 3·875) + (6 × 2·125) = (23·25 + 12·75) = 36 = B C² ; therefore, $\sqrt{36}$ = 6 = B C.

Out of these facts the following questions arise :—Is B N to N C in the ratio of 16 to 9 ? Is B N to N C in the ratio of 31 to 17 ? Or, are both these ratios fallacious ? It is self-evident that both cannot be true. These matters are within the scope, and ought to command the attention of, the British Association ; but if any gentleman were to attempt to deal with them in Section A of the Association, he would most assuredly be insulted.

I had written so far when I received the following communi-tion :—

Sir,

On the other side is a solution of your problem, without calling in the aid of the 6th Book, or the doctrine of similar triangles. I think there is no flaw in the process.

SOLUTION.

By hypothesis, $A B = 4a$ and $B C = 3a$.

∴. By Euclid, Prop. 47, Book 1, $A C = 5a$.

Area of triangle $A B C = \dfrac{A B \times B C}{2}$ also $= \dfrac{A C \times D B}{2}$

∴. $A B \times B C = A C \times D B$

$4a \times 3a = 5a \times D B$

∴. $D B = \tfrac{12}{5}a$.

But $B D C$ is a right-angled triangle.

∴. $B C^2 - B D^2 = D C^2$

$9a^2 - \tfrac{144}{25}a^2 = D C^2$

$\tfrac{81}{25}a^2 = D C^2$

$\tfrac{9}{5}a = D C$

Area of triangle $B D C = \dfrac{B D \times D C}{2}$ also $= \dfrac{B C \times D N}{2}$

∴. $B D \times D C = B C \times D N$

$\tfrac{12}{5}(a) \times \tfrac{9}{5}(a) = 3a \times D N$

∴. $D N = \tfrac{36}{25}(a)$

$B N = \sqrt{(B D^2 - D N^2)} = \sqrt{(\tfrac{144}{25}a^2) - \tfrac{1296}{625}a^2} = \tfrac{48}{25}a$

And, $N C = 3a - \tfrac{48}{25}a = \tfrac{27}{25}a$

∴. $B N : N C :: 48 : 27 :: 16 : 9$.

Yours, &c.,

X. Y. Z.

4th July, 1870.

X. Y. Z. arrives at the same conclusion as Gibbons, Garbett, and Miller as to the ratio of $B N$ to $N C$, but by a somewhat different "process." X. Y. Z. and Gibbons concur, in making $A D = 6\text{·}4$ and $D C = 3\text{·}6$, when $A B = 8$. But, $D N = 3$ by construction, and by computation $B N = 3\text{·}875$, and $N C = 2\text{·}125$, when $B C = 6$. Now, the "process" of X. Y. Z. would make $D N = 2\text{·}88$, $B N = 3\text{·}84$, and $N C = 2\text{·}16$. But, $B N = M D$, and $D N = M B$; and, by Euclid, Prop. 8, Book 6, $M D = \sqrt{15}$ when $M B = 3$. Can $B N$ and $M D$, which are opposite sides of the parallelogram $M B N D$, have different arithmetical values? Can $D N$ and $M B$, which are also opposite sides of the parallelogram $M B N D$, have different arithmetical values. Gibbons fancies he gets over this difficulty, by boldly asserting that $M D$ is not perpendicular to $A B$, and so upsets the fixed value of A M, making A M = 5·12, and consequently M B = 2·88. X. Y. Z. carefully omits all reference to the parallelogram M B N D, and this parallelogram is essential to the proof of the correctness of my solution of the problem.

The foregoing remarks will be plain enough to any honest mathematician, if he give what follows his careful consideration.

DIAGRAM.

With A B as perpendicular, describe the right-angled triangle A B C, making the sides A B and B C in the ratio of 8 to 6. Divide A B into two parts, A M and M B, so that A M shall be to M B in the ratio of 5 to 3. From the point M draw the straight line M D, perpendicular to A B, and, therefore, parallel to B C, to meet A C the hypothenuse of the triangle A B C in the point D, and join D B. From the point D draw the straight line D N perpendicular to B C, and, there-

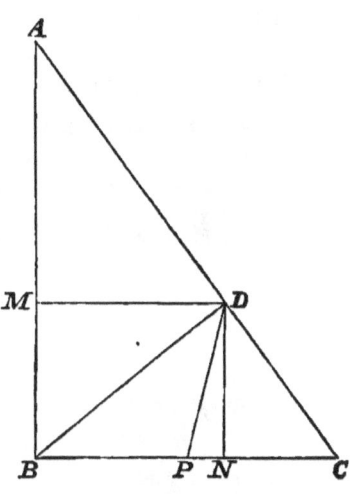

fore, parallel to A B, to meet B C the hypothenuse of the triangle B D C in the point N. Bisect B C in P, and join D P.

In the construction of this geometrical figure we avoid the introduction of a circle and all reference to a circle.

Let B C the hypothenuse of the right-angled triangle B D C = Χ ξ ς'—that is, the number of the Apocalyptic beast = 666.

It is self-evident that the whole line B C is divided into two equal parts B P and P C, and two unequal parts B N and N C. It is also self-evident that B N is divided into two unequal parts B P and P N.

PROBLEM.

Find the *exact* ratio expressed in whole numbers between B P and P N, and between B N and N C.

SOLUTION.

$$\frac{B\,C}{2} = \frac{666}{2} = 333 = B\,P$$

5

$\frac{1}{\pi}$ (BP) $= \frac{333}{24} = $ 13·875, and, 7(13·875) $= $ 97·125 $= $ P N

∴ B P + P N $= $ 333 + 97·125 $= $ 430·125 $= $ B N

But, B C is bisected in P.

∴ P C — P N $= $ 333 — 97·125 $= $ 235·875 $= $ N C

∴ BN + NC = 430·125 + 235·875 = 666 = the given value of BC.

Hence : B P : P N :: 24 : 7

that is, 333 : 97·125 :: 24 : 7

and, BN : N C :: 31 : 17

that is, 430·125 : 235·875 :: 31 : 17

And it follows, that D N : D P : : p : c, where p denotes the perimeter of a regular hexagon, and c denotes the circumference of its circumscribing circle. I think X. Y. Z. will find no flaw in the process.

Saturday afternoon's post brought me the following extraordinary communication :—

185, Islington, Liverpool, 9th July, 1870.

DEAR SIR,

Before you republished my articles on the "Curiosities of Mathematics," I informed you that I valued the copyright at twenty guineas for each article, and that (unless you immediately accepted some lower terms which I then proposed) I should expect payment at that rate.

You did not accept the terms which I propòsed, but you did deliberately use my property with full cognizanceof the price which I put upon it, (as you have since admitted in one of your Letters to the *Leader.*)

I am happy to be assured that no question can arise as to the intrinsic value of my papers. I had a right to put what price I chose upon them : just as you might put any fancy price on any article of yours which I desired to make use of. As you were cognizant of my price before publication, I have no hesitation in asking you to remit to me the full amount.

I may add, that if you desire any more articles of the same character at the same price, I shall be happy to supply them, as I am anxious to raise funds to pay off debts on my church and schools.

I am, dear Sir,

Yours faithfully,

W. ALLEN WHITWORTH.

This bark seems very like the bark of a cur. Mr. Whitworth is quite at liberty to bite, by instructing his solicitor to take proceedings against me to enforce payment of his demand. I have given another problem in this Letter, and I can assure Mr. Whitworth that certain leading members of "The British Association for the Advancement of Science" would be delighted to find an article of his in the *Liverpool Leader*, proving, by means of orthodox and recognised systems, that my solution of the problem is "*a mockery, a delusion, and a snare.*" If Mr. Whitworth will insert such an article, I shall be happy to subscribe twenty guineas to a fund, to enable him "to pay off the debts on his church and schools."

Mr. Gibbons has not replied to my Letter of the 25th June, which appeared in the *Leader* of the 2nd inst., neither have I a reply from Mr. Garbett to my letter to him which appeared in your last week's number. It would seem as if both had become "dumb dogs" that "cannot bark." Both are silenced, but neither has the *mathematical* honesty to throw up the sponge, and admit that he is beaten in a fair battle. In this Letter I have given the British Association something worthy of attention at its forthcoming meeting; but I may tell you that, as a confraternity, I have found the members of that body to be men possessed of heads so crammed with uncommon sense, "*that there is not a cranny left for reasoning to get in at*," and I shall not again lay myself open to insult by offering to read a Paper in Section A.

In conclusion : It will be self-evident to any reader, if only a school-boy, that Gibbons, Garbett, Miller, and X. Y. Z. (why had the latter not the moral courage to give his name?) make the ratio between the lengths of two unequal lines the same as the ratio between the areas of squares on two other unequal lines in the diagram. Nothing can be more absurd, and yet such is the conclusion arrived at by the Mathematician's application of Mathematics to Geometry. It is sufficient that I have caught in my trap five "blind mice," and I shall not notice any further Letters, whether public, private, or anonymous, unless and until your contributors Whitworth and Gibbons have either admitted the correctness of my solution of the problem given in the *Leader* of the 11th June, or proved it to be fallacious.

I am, Sir,

Yours obediently,

JAMES SMITH.

BARKELEY HOUSE, SEAFORTH,
11th July, 1870.

FROM THE "LIVERPOOL LEADER," JULY 23RD, 1870.

CURIOSITIES OF MATHEMATICS.

TO THE EDITOR OF THE LIVERPOOL LEADER.

SIR,

The Letter under the above title, which appeared in the *Leader* of Saturday, I intended to be the last of the series, but my correspondence of last week is of such importance, that I must ask you to give it a place in your next number.

ALEX. ED. MILLER TO J. S.

SIR,

As you have mentioned my name in your Letter to the *Leader* of Saturday, perhaps you will be good enough to insert the following reply to your " solution " :—

P N is not $= \frac{7}{71}$ (B P), but $= \frac{7}{75}$ (B P).

For, $BN \times BC = BD^2$

and, $\frac{BD}{DC} = \frac{AB}{BC} = \frac{3}{4}$

$\therefore DC^2 = \frac{9}{16}(BD^2)$: $BC^2 = BD^2 (1 \times \frac{9}{16}) = \frac{25}{16}(BD^2)$

$\therefore BN = \frac{16}{25}(BC) = \frac{32}{25}(BP)$

$PN = (\frac{32}{25} - 1) BP = \frac{7}{25}(BP)$

Now, if $BC = 6$

$B N = \frac{16}{25} \times 6 = 3.84$

$N C = \frac{9}{25} \times 6 = 2.16.$

Q. E. D.

In the question given in Saturday's *Leader* in Greek numerals, I suspect that s' is a misprint for ς'. If s' is right, the answer is 3·8763 very nearly. If ς' is right, the answer is = 3·125.

I cannot guess what "orthodox theory" would render the solution of the problem given in June 11 an utter impossibility ; to me it seemed a very simple deduction from Euclid, Prop. 47, Book 1, and Prop. 8, Book 6.

Your obedient servant,

ALEX. ED. MILLER.

11*th July*, 1870.

J. S. TO ALEX. ED. MILLER.

SIR,

In reply to your favour of yesterday, I beg to inform you that the only Letter of yours to the Editor of the *Liverpool Leader* that I have seen is the one that appeared in that Journal of the 25th June. You may have sent him the supposed solution of my problem that you now give me, but it is the first time I have seen it.

Let A B be a straight line divided into two unequal parts A M and M B in the ratio of 5 to 3. With A B as perpendicular describe the right-angled triangle A B C, making A B to B C in the ratio of 8 to 6. From the point M draw a straight line perpendicular to A B, and, therefore, parallel to B C, to meet A C the hypothenuse of the triangle A B C in the point D, and join D B. From the angle D draw a straight

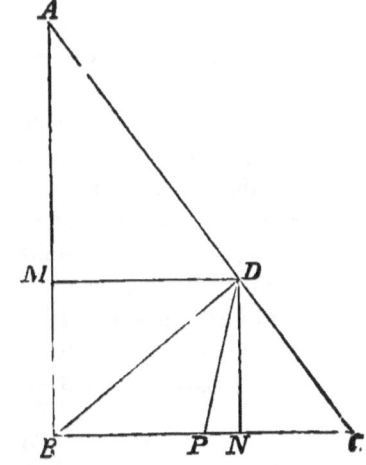

line parallel to A B, and therefore, perpendicular to B C, to meet B C the hypothenuse of the right-angled triangle B D C in the point N. Bisect B C in P, and join D P.

If you bisect A B in O, and with O as centre and O A or O B as radius describe a circle, you will find that the circumference of the circle will not cut A C the hypothenuse of the triangle A B C in the point D, but in a point nearer C.*

$$\text{Let } A B = 8.$$

Then : By construction :

$$\tfrac{3}{4}(A\ B) = \tfrac{3}{4}(8) = 6 = B\ C$$
$$\tfrac{5}{8}(A\ B) = \tfrac{5}{8}(8) = 5 = A\ M$$
$$\text{and, } \tfrac{3}{8}(A\ B) = \tfrac{3}{8}(8) = 3 = M\ B$$

But, B C is bisected in P.

$$\therefore\ B\ P = P\ C = M\ B = 3.$$

By Euclid, Prop. 8, Book 6.

$$A\ M \times M\ B = 5 \times 3 = 15 = M\ D^2$$

But B N = M D, for they are opposite sides of the parallelogram M B N D.

$\therefore$ B N = $\sqrt{15}$ = 3·872. &c., and is greater than 3·84, which you make the value of B N in the figure in my Letter to the *Leader* of June 11.

Hence :

$$B\ N = \tfrac{31}{48} \times 6 = 3\text{·}875$$
$$N\ C = \tfrac{17}{48} \times 6 = 2\text{·}125$$
$$\therefore\ B\ N : N\ C :: 3\text{·}875 : 2\text{·}125$$
$$\therefore\ 31 : 17 :: 3\text{·}875 : 2\text{·}125$$

And the product of the means is equal to the product of the extremes.

You will find that A M D and D N C are not similar triangles.

The symbol to which you refer is somewhat unshapely, but stands for the Greek numeral 6, and your answer 3·125 is correct.

I yesterday gave the Editor of the *Leader* the MSS. of a Letter which will appear in next Saturday's number, of which I will send you a copy. With that Letter I intended to conclude the series on "Curiosities of Mathematics ;" but if, after perusing it, you still wish your Letter of yesterday to appear in the *Leader*, please say so, and I will have it inserted with my reply in the following week's number.

Your obedient Servant,

12th July, 1870.   JAMES SMITH.

* This paragraph contains an absurd assertion, "without any attempt at proof."   J. S.

P.S.—I think I sent you a copy of the *Liverpool Leader* of the 2nd inst., but I suspect that you have not read a Letter of mine that appeared in it. I send you another copy by this post.

————

ALEX. ED. MILLER TO J. S.

SIR,

I am obliged by yours of yesterday. I only sent a solution of your problem of June 11, which is the one you allude to. My Letter of Monday was called forth by yours which appeared in the *Leader* of July 9, in which you say that " Gibbons, Garbett, and Miller fell into the trap" you had set by answering that problem by the proportion 16 : 9. I still maintain that 16 : 9 is the true answer to the problem of June 11, and I should wish my Letter of Monday to appear, unless you formally and publicly withdraw the expression above quoted. To-day you send me a totally new construction, in which B D C is no longer a right-angled triangle, and therefore your solution is wrong, because $AM \times MB$ is not $= MD^2$ (BDA not being a right angle), and therefore BN, which is $= MD$, is not $\sqrt{15}$. If it were, you would have $BN : NC :: \sqrt{15} : (\sqrt{5} - \sqrt{3}) \sqrt{3}$, which cannot be expressed in whole numbers. You yourself practically admit that B D C is not a right angle when you say, the circle described with A B as diameter will not meet A C in D, but a point somewhat nearer C. That is true. Let that point be E, and join B E. Now, B E A is the angle in a semi-circle.

∴ B E D is a right-angled triangle.

∴ B D C is less than a right-angle.

∴ MD^2 is greater than A M × M B.

The true answer to your new diagram, which is even simpler than the original one, is :—

$BN : NC :: AD : DC :: AM : MB : 5 : 3.$ Q. E. D.

If you publish your Letter of yesterday, please add this to it ; if not, you can do as you please about it.

Your obedient Servant,

ALEX. ED. MILLER.

13*th July*, 1870.

J. S. TO ALEX. ED. MILLER.

SIR,

I am obliged by yours of the 13th inst., but not more obliged than surprised. The truth is, you attempt to reconcile Geometry with your notion of Mathematics, losing sight of the fact that Mathematics must necessarily harmonise with the *exact* science of Geometry ; and when rightly applied, can never be inconsistent with practical Geometry.

Take the figure in my Letter to you of the 12th inst. From the angle A draw a straight line parallel to D B to meet another straight line drawn from the angle B parallel to A D in a point F, and so construct a rectangular parallelogram A F B D. A B will be a diagonal of the parallelogram and divide it into two similar and equal right-angled triangles. Again: From the angle B draw a straight line parallel to D C to meet another straight line drawn from the angle C parallel to B D in a point G, and so construct a rectangular parallelogram D B G C. B C will be a diagonal of the parallelogram and divide it into two similar and equal right-angled triangles. Surely these facts will convince you of the absurdity of your assertion, that "B D C is less than a right angle ;" and I cannot help thinking you will see how you and others have been *caught in a trap*.

It is assumed by Mathematicians that straight lines drawn to points in A C, from any point in A B parallel to B C, and from any point in B C parallel to A B, will produce two right-angled triangles similar to the triangle A B C. *This is not true*, and you will find that A M D, A B C, and D N C are not similar triangles in the figure in my Letter of the 12th inst.

I have never said that any Proposition of Euclid is not true under *any* circumstances. What I have said, and what I maintain, is, that certain Propositions of Euclid are inconsistent with certain other Propositions, and are, therefore, not of general and universal application in practical Geometry, and, consequently, are not true, under *all* circumstances.

Now, with reference to the figure in my Letter in the *Liverpool Leader* of June 11, you might have made out, by a certain method of computation, that A M $= 5\cdot12$ and B M $= 2\cdot88$ when A B the diameter of the circle = 8; making A D = 6·4, D C = 3·6, B N = 3·84, and N C = 2·16; and, if this were true, it would follow, that A M D, A B C, and D N C would be similar right-angled triangles, having the sides that contain the right angle in the ratio of 3 to 4.

Therefore, $A B^2 \times B C^2 = (A D + D C)^2$

and, $D B^2 \times D C^2 = (B N + N C)^2$

       $\therefore D P^2 \times P B^2 = 2(P B \times P N) = D B^2$

From these facts other results follow, which I may leave you to trace out.

In conclusion: Your Letters and my answers shall be inserted in the next number of the *Liverpool Leader*.

Your obedient Servant,
J. S.

16th July, 1870.

We shall see what Mr. Miller makes of this communication. If he answer it, I shall have another Letter for you, with which I shall certainly conclude my series on " Curiosities of Mathematics."

I am, Sir, yours obediently,
JAMES SMITH.

BARKELEY HOUSE, SEAFORTH,
      18th July, 1870.

FROM THE " LIVERPOOL LEADER," JULY 30TH, 1870.

CURIOSITIES OF MATHEMATICS.

TO THE EDITOR OF THE LIVERPOOL LEADER.

SIR,

      I have received several communications during the past week, but it is not necessary to trouble you with the whole of them. It is sufficient to give you the following correspondence:—

X. Y. Z. TO JAMES SMITH.

X. Y. Z. takes exception to two points in your communication appearing in the *Leader* of the 16th instant. Referring to your figure, you say that the triangle B D C is a right-angled triangle. You do not prove that it is so, and it can easily be proved (to my satisfaction at least) that it is not.

Again :—In your solution you say (without a shadow of proof) that $B N = \frac{7}{24} (B P)$; and assuming this, you have of course no difficulty in proving that $B N : N C :: (24 + 7) : (24 - 7) :: 31 : 17$.

Without some common basis of argument it is of course useless attempting to argue ; but if you admit (and I should think of all men you would be the last to deny) the universality of the simple rule that the area of a plane rectilinear triangle is one-half the product of the base and the perpendicular upon the base, you may easily satisfy yourself that the proportion you gave as the supposed solution of your problem is not correct.

Referring again to your figure—

Area of triangle A B C $= \dfrac{A \times B}{2} = \dfrac{8 \times 6}{2} = 24.$

But, triangle A B C = triangle A D B + triangle B D C.

Now, area of triangle B D C $= \dfrac{BC \times DN}{2} = \dfrac{6 \times 3}{2} = 9.$

$\therefore$ Area of triangle A D B $= 24 - 9 = 15.$

But, area of triangle ADB $= \dfrac{A B \times M D}{2} = \dfrac{8 M D}{2} = 4 M D.$

$\therefore 4 M D = 15$, and $M D = \frac{15}{4}.$

But, B N = M D, by construction.

$\therefore B N = \frac{15}{4}.$

And, since B P = 3, P N will $= \frac{3}{4}$ and N C $= \frac{9}{4}.$

$\therefore B N : N C :: 15 : 9.$

I need hardly say that the figure so constructed is materially different from that formerly constructed with the aid of the circle ; and if in your figure of Saturday you bisect A B in O, and with O B as a radius describe a circle, such circle will not pass through the point D ; for, if D O be joined, the line D O will not be equal to O B, which it would be if D were a point in the circumference.

18*th July*, 1870.

X. Y. Z. fails to perceive that A B C and D N C are *not* similar triangles. Mr. Miller, in his Letter of the 11th inst., assumes A B C and D N C to be similar triangles, and I threw him off the scent in my Letter of the 12th inst. (these Letters appear in your last number) by suggesting the argument of X Y Z.

By hypothesis, let A M = 5·12 and M B = 2·88.

Then :
$$A M + M B = 5·12 + 2·88 = 8 = A B$$
$$A B \times A M = 8 \times 5·12 = 40·96 = A D^2$$
$$\therefore A D = \sqrt{40·96} = 6·4.$$
$$A B \times M B = 8 \times 2·88 = 23·04 = B D^2$$
$$\therefore B D = \sqrt{23·04} = 4·8.$$
$$B C^2 - B D^2 = 6^2 - 4·8^2 = 36 - 23·04 = 12·96 = D C^2$$
$$\therefore D C = \sqrt{12·96} = 3·6.$$

Hence : A B × B C = (A D × D B) + (B D × D C), and this would make A B C and D N C similar right-angled triangles.

Mathematicians have never discovered that if the length of a straight line be represented by $\sqrt{15}$, its true length is $3 + \frac{7}{24}(3) = 3·875$, and not 3·872, &c., the extracted root of $\sqrt{15}$.

ALEX. ED. MILLER TO J. S.

DEAR SIR,

I do not see that our correspondence can be usefully continued, but I owe it to your courtesy to answer your last. I admit that Mathematics can never " be inconsistent with practical Geometry," which, indeed, *is* one of the phases of Mathematics, and it is on that very account that I maintain, that a proposition shown, as yours has been shown, to err against one or more of the fundamental principles of Geometry, can never be set on its legs by any amount of Arithmetic. In the construction you suggest in your last, the parallelograms will not be rectangles, and therefore nothing to the point. In opposition to you, I maintain, and till you show me specific instances in Euclid to the contrary, will continue to believe, that there is no Proposition of Euclid inconsistent, under any circumstances, with any other, and that no plane rectilinear figure can be drawn inconsistent in any particular with any Proposition in, or necessary deduction from, elementary Geometry (*i.e.*, Euclid).

It is not assumed by Mathematicians that straight lines drawn from any point in A B parallel to B C, &c., cut the triangle A B C into similar triangles ; this is distinctly proved in Euclid, Prop. 2, Book 6, and is universally true.

All your work in reference to the figures in the *Liverpaol Leader* require the concurrent existence of two inconsistent postulates : (1) B D C = a right-angled triangle, and (2) A M : M B : : 5 : 3. I have shown that these cannot co-exist (when A B : B C : : 8 : 6) unless you can have either (1) a plane triangle the sum of whose angles is greater than two right angles, or (2) a semi-circle containing an angle less than a right angle. These are both impossibilities, therefore your postulates are mutually destructive. *Utrum harum maris accipe*, when accepted it proves the other false.

Your obedient servant,
ALEX. ED. MILLER.

24, OLD BUILDINGS, LINCOLN'S INN,
  18*th July*, 1870.

P.S.—What you say I " might have shown," is precisely what I did show you.

A. E. M.

J. S. TO ALEX. ED. MILLER.

DEAR SIR,
            I am in receipt of yours of the 18th, which has surprised me more than did your favour of the 13th inst.

You admit that " Mathematics can never be inconsistent with practical Geometry," and I as freely admit (1) that the three angles of a plane triangle are together equal to two right angles ; and (2) that any two straight lines drawn from the extremities of a diameter of a circle to a point in the circumference, will produce a right-angled triangle. Like you, " I do not see that our correspondence can be usefully continued."

Yesterday morning's post brought me a diagram from Mr. E. L. Garbett. I acknowledged its receipt, and send you the diagram herewith. Take ample time to carefully examine it, and then please return it. I shall direct your attention to some facts with reference to it, and with this our controversy must terminate.

A B C is a right-angled triangle, with the base B C bisected in P, and Mr. Garbett makes the sides B C and A B, that contain the right angle, 600 and 800, making A C the hypothenuse 1000. The sides of the triangle A B C he divides into parts, and gives the arithmetical value of the separate parts. In the figure there are two parallelograms, each of which is divided by a diagonal into two similar and equal right-angled triangles. The sides of the small right-angled triangle of which D′D is the hypothenuse, are 9, 12, and 15, and it follows, that this triangle and the triangle A B C are similar, but not equal, right-angled triangles ; and whether you and Mr. Garbett can, or can not, see it, it also follows, that the angles D′ and D in the triangles B D′ C and B D C are right angles.* The triangle A B C and the triangle A M′ D′ are similar right-angled triangles, having the sides that contain the right angle in the ratio of 3 to 4. The triangles A M D and A M′ D′ are both within the circle, but the angle D of only one of them touches it.

Mr. Garbett is obviously not satisfied, or he would not have been at the trouble of constructing and sending me the diagram.

Faithfully yours,

J. S.

BARKELEY HOUSE, SEAFORTH,
20*th July*, 1870.

———

J. S. TO ALEX. ED. MILLER.

DEAR SIR,

Your favour of the 19th inst. came to hand last evening. If I were to answer it and similar communications, our correspondence might never terminate.

* Mr. Miller was quick to detect the absurdity of the assertion :—" The angle D′ and D in the triangles B D′ C and B D C are right angles," but failed to discover the glaring absurdities involved in the arithmetical values Mr. Garbett puts on the lines in the diagram.

I may tell you, that in my published works I have proved many things by the Sines of angles, and also by Logarithms.*

Having dropped you and Mr. Garbett into a quagmire of geometrical inconsistency, contradiction, and confusion, I must leave you there. My last series of letters in the *Liverpool Leader* on " Curiosities of Mathematics " will shortly appear in the form of a pamphlet.

Faithfully yours,

J. S.

BARKELEY HOUSE, SEAFORTH,
    21*st July*, 1870.

———

One of the greatest blunders of Mathematicians *is*, that ot making the *geometrical* and *trigonometrical* sines of angles the same. Mr. Alex. Ed. Miller fell into this blunder in a Letter of his which appeared in the *Correspondent* more than four years ago. Unequal angles may have a common sine *geometrically*, but never *trigono-metrically*. Unequal triangles may *trigonometrically* have the same sines and cosines ; indeed, if in unequal right-angled triangles the angles are equal, which is not an impossibility, the trigonometrical sines and cosines of the angles will necessarily be equal. One of Mr. Miller's assumptions is, that triangles are similar if the angles are equal, although the ratios of side to side are unequal.

I shall have no more Letters for you on " Curiosities of Mathematics," unless and until your contributor, the Rev. W. Allen Whitworth, renews his.

I am, Sir,

Yours obediently,

JAMES SMITH.

BARKELEY HOUSE, SEAFORTH,
    25*th July*, 1870.

———

When Mr. Miller returned Mr. Garbett's diagram, he sent with it the following communication :—

* In his Letter Mr. Miller introduced a fallacious argument, founded on the trigonometrical Sines of Angles.

24, OLD BUILDINGS, LINCOLN'S INN,
26th July, 1870.

DEAR SIR,

I return Mr. Garbett's diagram, which seems all right.

If you do not see that your construction, coupled with your admissions : (1) that " any two straight lines drawn from the extremities of a diameter of a circle to a point in the circumference, will produce a right-angled triangle," and (2) that " if you bisect A B in O, and with O A or O B as radius describe a circle, the circumference will not cut A C in the point D, but in a point nearer C," amounts to saying, that from the point B two distinct perpendiculars can be drawn to A C, one to the point D, and the other to the plane where A C meets the circumference. In other words, that in Mr. Garbett's diagram, A D B is a right-angled triangle, whether the D is red or black. (In his diagram Mr. Garbett put some of the lines and letters in red ink, and others in black.) If you can shew by any abstract reasoning in the world, geometrical or otherwise, that two distinct perpendiculars can be drawn from the same point to *any* straight line whatever, you may earn the right to talk of having left your opponents in a quagmire of inconsistencies ; but until some better proof of this is given than the reiterated assertion that " it follows, whether Mr. Garbett can see it or not," you may possibly believe such a thing to be possible, but you will be the only man in England, who knows what an angle is, who will do so.

I should not have troubled you with this but for your note in Saturday's *Leader :*—" We shall see what Mr. Miller makes of this communication." And you have seen it, and may make what you can of it.

Your obedient servant,
ALEX. ED. MILLER.

P.S.—I do not understand the distinction you seem to draw between Geometry and Mathematics ; at any rate, I have throughout, except when I consented to follow you into Arithmetic—been dealing with Geometry only, and that of the simplest kind.

A. E. M.

For an answer to Mr. Miller's P.S. I may refer him to the concluding part of my Letter in the *Liverpool Leader* of July 30th, (see pages 41-6). I admit, that unequal straight lines drawn from the same point, can never be perpendicular to the same straight line. By suggesting a false hypothesis, and by making an absurd assertion, I seem to have disturbed Mr. Miller's equanimity, and thrown him altogether off the right scent. Mathematician like, he is quick to detect a fallacy, but apparently incompetent to comprehend a new geometrical truth, however stringently demonstrated.

The Reader will observe from dates, that Mr. Miller kept Mr. Garbett's diagram a full week, and I may fairly infer, that he gave it a careful examination. It is obvious that it did not suggest anything new to him.

The annexed diagram is much smaller, but in all other respects similar to Mr. Garbett's. He did not give me his method of constructing the diagram, and I can only conjecture it from his values of the various lines. He may have constructed it in the following way:—

Draw the straight line B P and produce it to N', making P N' $= \frac{1}{4}$ (B P). Produce P N' to C, making N'C $=$ 3 (P N'). From the point B draw B A perpendicular to B C, making B A $= \frac{1}{3}$ (B C), and join A C. Bisect A B in O, and with O as centre and O A or O B as radius, describe the semi-circle A D B. From the point D where the semi-circle cuts A C, draw D M perpendicular to A B, and therefore parallel to B C. Join D O and D P, and from the point D draw D N perpendicular to B C, and therefore parallel to A B. From N' draw a straight line perpendicular to B C to meet A C the hypothenuse of the right-angled triangle A B C in the point D', and from

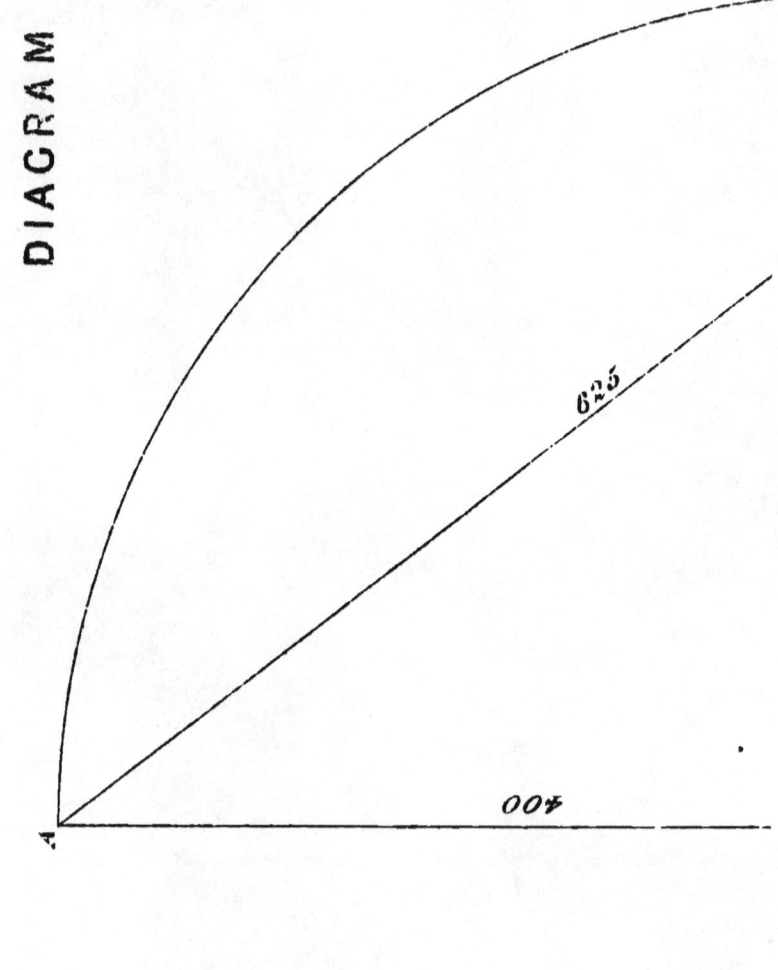

DIAGRAM

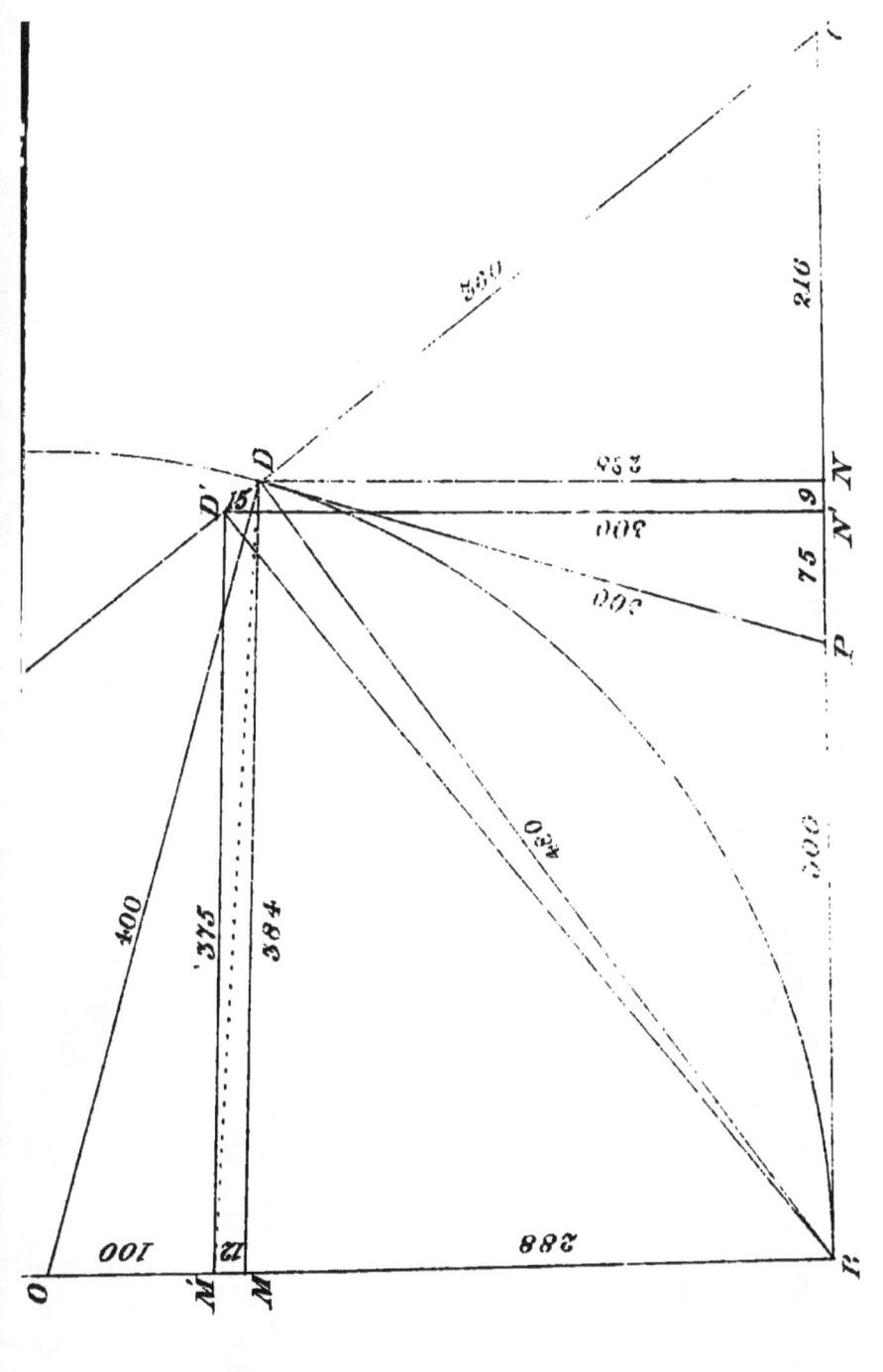

D' draw the straight line D' M' parallel to D M. Join B D and B D.'

My method of constructing the diagram is as follows :

I first draw two straight lines of indefinite length at right angles to each other, making B the right angle. I then open my compasses at random, and from the angle B mark off six equal parts together equal to B C, and eight of such parts together equal to A B, join A C, and bisect B C in P. The rest of the construction must be the same as Mr. Garbett's, whatever we make our starting point.

Mr. Garbett makes A B = 800, B P = 300, = B C 600, and A C = 1000 : by construction, and so far we are agreed : that is to say, we are agreed, that A B is to B C in the ratio of 8 to 6, and A C to B C in the ratio of 10 to 6, by construction ; and no amount of Mathematics can upset these ratios.

Now, any person may take a pair of compasses, and with B as centre and B P as radius, describe a circle. The circumference of such circle will cut the line A B in the point M, and it follows, that B M must equal B P, for they are radii of the circle. But, Mr. Garbett makes B P = 300, by construction ; and by computation makes B M only = 288. Again : Mr. Garbett makes D' M' = D' C = 375. With D' as centre and D' M' as radius, describe a circle. The circumference of such circle will not pass through the point C, but through a point in the line D' C nearer D'. Here again, computation is not in harmony with construction. Is it conceivable that anything could be more absurd ?

Mr. Miller says of Mr. Garbett's diagram, "it seems all right;" which surely means, that he agrees with

Mr. Garbett, as to the arithmetical values he has put on the various lines of which his geometrical figure is composed. De Morgan, Whitworth, and all other "*recognised Mathematicians*, attempt to make Geometry fit their Mathematics, instead of endeavouring to make Mathematics harmonize with Geometry. Mr. Garbett's diagram is the best illustration of this fact that has ever come under my observation.

I might point out absurdity upon absurdity with reference to this remarkable geometrical figure. Why should I? In Geometry, one *reductio ad absurdum* demonstration is as good as a thousand. I have given two. X. Y. Z. (can X. Y. Z be J. T. T. who wrote on this subject some years ago, and whose Letters appeared in the *Daily Post* under the sobriquet of Pi) Miller, Garbett, and Gibbons, might readily furnish many more, if they could but get rid of prejudice, and go *honestly* to work. I have done my duty! Let Mathematicians and the British Association do theirs.

JAMES SMITH.

BARKELEY HOUSE, SEAFORTH,
4th August, 1870.

ERRATA.

Page 24 : 11th line from bottom—For B N = M B : read B N = M D.

Page 29 : 11th line from bottom—For by construction 5 : read by construction = 5.

ANDREW AND DAVID RUSSELL, PRINTERS, LIVERPOOL